I0661635

Richard Whieldon Baddeley

Cassandra

And other Poems

Richard Whieldon Baddeley

Cassandra
And other Poems

ISBN/EAN: 9783744765251

Printed in Europe, USA, Canada, Australia, Japan

Cover: Foto ©Andreas Hilbeck / pixelio.de

More available books at **www.hansebooks.com**

CASSANDRA: AND OTHER POEMS.

CASSANDRA:

AND OTHER POEMS.

BY

R. WHIELDON BADDELEY,

AUTHOR OF " THE SQUIRE OF CHAPEL
DARESFIELD," ETC.

LONDON:

BELL AND DALDY, YORK STREET,

COVENT GARDEN.

1869.

IN the poem " CASSANDRA " the author has not thought it necessary to pay strict regard to any of the contradictory legends which affect his characters.

CONTENTS.

Contents.

CASSANDRA.

PERSONS OF THE DRAMA.

CASSANDRA.

ŒNONE.

PRIAM.

PARIS.

CORÆBUS.

A Grecian Soldier.

CHORUS of Trojan Women.

SCENE—Troy and Mount Ida.

TIME—First just before, and then during and just after, the Siege of Troy.

CASSANDRA.

ACT I. SCENE I.

CASSANDRA.

 BEAUTEOUS hour of eve! sweeter
to me
Than e'er thou art to tired ox or hind!
O intense, calm, tumult-appeasing soul
Of purple-skirted twilight, into mine
Infused, and bringing to me sadness, or
Its unsubstantial shadow, till my eyes
Know tears more sweet than smiles, and gentle as
The dew which is as Heaven now wept for earth;

For **Ares has** made earth red as **the set**
Of sun, or yon Sigeum's marble cliffs,
While, as the storm from where the halcyons fly,
He keeps aloof from happy Ilion.

How, piercing through yon cushions of rose-
cloud,
Gleams yonder star-point! so, I think, my soul
Is brilliant above pleasures which it loves;
And as Polyxena is a fair flower
Of earth, of the paler kind,—as, for compare,
Œnone brings to mind the buoyant breeze
Happy to murmur under a blue sky,
As she to sing her heart's abundance 'neath
The heaven of Paris's love; so—for in me
Is something not of earth, yet loving earth—
I am as yonder colour-cinctured star.

How weary of earth and earth's must he have
been,

The hero doom'd to labours vain as vast;

Or he, the greater Titan, whose proud lip

Æons of agony on Caucasus

Might blanch, but could not writhe: upon *my* lips

Are only smiles, and in my soul delight;

And palace and not prison to me is earth,

Vivid with light, and passionate with life;

From where, majestic, the great mountain soars,

Like its own eagles, almost to the sun,

To where the rivulet chafes around a stone,

And centuries may make loud cities dumb,

But still that rivulet chafes around the stone:

Yes; ever with me is the glory of

The soaring mountain and the rushing stream,

The restlessness of clouds that know all hues,

The rest of arching heaven that knows but one!

Enter PARIS.

Paris! Œnone but this afternoon

Show'd us your sail.

PARIS.

Its yard you surely mean,

The sail is not yet spread.

CASS.

You made her think

It was.

PARIS.

Because I wish'd her so to think.

Howe'er, my anchor will I weigh to-night,

So balmy is the breeze, so bright the stars !

CASS.

Paris ! she loves you, and you have loved her ;

Constant is she, you false as she is fair.

PARIS.

She is fair and sweet, and constant to herself.

CASS.

What mean you, Paris ? constant to herself ?

PARIS.

Why, if a man acquires a bag of gold,

Deserves he more by keeping it, than if

He spend and have it gone? Nay, in men's

    mouths

The spendthrift better than the miser fares :

So, for this constancy in love, it means

That, having found what one desires, one grieves

To lose it ; merit there is none in this

As I think.

CASS.

You think basely, stupidly.

PARIS.

Look you, Cassandra, as my sail will flap

To separate us soon, I now transfer

To you what others' generosity

Has made me somewhat affluent in—advice :

You are my favourite sister.

CASS.

Rather say
The sole one of your sisters you endure.

PARIS.

Because I bear a brain, and so do you;
Because I am like you in spirit, or was once;
We are wingèd creatures, you and I; not like
The dull ants round us, who so busily course
With burdens up and down this ant-hill earth.

CASS.

But I love human kind, and have no scorn;
The ant is honourable in his place,
And usefuller than is the butterfly,
Who lives but to be weary of the flowers.
There's not in all the cities of the world
The poorest household that to its own mirth
And its own mourning were more quick than I,
Could I but be among them and their words!

PARIS.

Should man, this worm who crawls, and stings,
        and dies,

This miserable laughing-stock of gods,

Created for a jest, but playing pranks

Worse than a jest, upon earth's stage, which has

The universe for amphitheatre ;—

Should man be honour'd, who for others cares

So little,—and so blindly for himself?

CASS.

There's something self-applausive in the vein
Of cynicism.

PARIS.

Something natural.

CASS.

But nothing true; the individuals

Of human kind care only for themselves,

You say; explain, then, how it comes about

That all who know her love Polyxena,

The lily, as the minstrels sing, of Troy;

She is not very wise or very fair,

Nor mirthful like Œnone, nor has wit

Like mine, that flashes pleasure, so they say;

A girl, though royal, scattereth not gifts;

Why is she loved of all, then, as she is?

PARIS.

Polyxena has a pretty face enough,

And not too pretty; then she has no foes,

For most of us hate others because all

Strive for the same ends in life's shouldering

      fight:

Polyxena wants nothing, does not strive,

Is always second where there are but two!

You name her lily truly, with the world

She deals as does the lily with the stream:

And much it flatters us to rule o'er those

Who, competent themselves, allow our reign.

Yes! your sweet instance should be mine, not

      yours.

But, look you here, Cassandra ; noble and pure

You are I know, and in your presence I

Have less of Paris than I have otherwhere ;

But this nobility and purity,

And this revealing of all glorious things

That shine betwixt the diamond of mid earth

And the high sun that crowns us of mid heaven,

To thine exulting and abounding youth

May seem a benison, my sister fair,

But is a curse, as was the splendid robe

Corinthian Glauce wore ; nor felt, until

She had dazzled her own eyes in it an hour,

Its poison.   I was once as you are now ;

I, also, search'd for immortality,

And found it, and I wearied of it ;—woe

To those who forestall heaven while on earth !

The love-locks which I curl and scent, and you

Laugh at, Cassandra, should be snakes to fit

The thoughts that pass behind the reveller's

    brow.

Cass.

O, it was not your rising made you fall;
I think that if you loved the song, it was
Because some siren sang it.

Paris.

                    In some shape
The curse will come, it matters not in what;
Prometheus suffers pain upon his rock
Not less than Sisyphus, who heaves his stone.

Cass.

Yet would I choose betwixt these pains to have
        one
Before the other.

Paris.

            Faith, too, so would I
Choose—to have neither. But the evening breeze
Gives life unto the waters' azure death.

Farewell, Cassandra ; mind thy spinning more,

As Priam would have thee, and thy dreaming

    less.

Here come my brown-faced sailors, on their lips

The freshening breeze ; farewell ! star after star

Pierces the purple of the summer night ;

And I, right weary of the babbling tongues

Of Ilion, and of Ida's bubbling brooks,

Am eager as my sail. Swift be my speed !

As by a petrel's wing would I be drawn

To pleasures, and to fortunes, and to Greece.

SCENE II.

CASSANDRA *sings.*

O TO a length unending
    Be drawn that flute-note rare,
Then to the lives we are spending
    It fitly might compare.

Lives that are all of pleasure,
    Which purples e'en our dreams;
O lightly goes our leisure
    Beside Scamander's streams!

Day follows day, but ever
    On Ilion's town divine,
Fair with the pride men sever
    From quarry and from mine,
Hill-terraced o'er its river,
    The suns unclouded shine!

—Shine o'er far Ida's masses,

  From base to summit blue,

O'er which no cloudlet passes

  To darken their deep hue.

The long Ionian summer!

  The day that never ends,

For with the bright new comer

  Its lingering light still blends!

Cities there be whose daughters

  Lament by streams that lave

But ruins red with slaughters

  And streets turn'd to a grave;

We weep not by our waters,

  Nor wish them Lethe's wave.

Coræbus! join the dance.

      CORÆBUS.

        Ah, is it done,

Thy singing? sure his minstrelsy who made

Trees follow him, had never power like thine.

CASS.

And sure the slenderest silverest bark'd birch

That 'mid the dancing forest footed it,

Ne'er went so lightly as thy plighted bride,

Whose white hands wait thine now, whene'er the

    dance

Flushes the lily of that gentle face,

Unlocks the fountain of that soft brown hair,

And shows that figure—an Ionian shaft

Rises not to its volutes gracefuller;

Surely thy plighted bride, Polyxena,

Is of the fair and happy Trojan girls

The fairest?

COR. (?)

I think not.

CASS.

Join thou the dance.

Cor.

And why are thy feet still?

Cass. (*smiling*).

　　　　　　To lighter forms
Than mine is given the dance; to me the song.

Cor.

I saw a statue of Calliope
Once; she sat pensive, with her broad brow lean'd
Upon one hand, the other hung, and held
Beside her white-stoled knee the lyric quill;
Grave was her face, yet genial; less severe
Her form than stately and yet with youth in it—
Her noble beauty seem'd to me like thine.

Cass.

The girls have stopp'd their strophe; 'tis for
　　　youths
To take their hands, and move adown the dance,

c

With swinging at their belts of golden swords;

Go, or Polyxena will hate me,—go!

> [*He goes, they dance, and all but* CORÆBUS
>
> *dance off.*

CORÆBUS.

Cassandra!

CASS.

　　　Wherefore fearest thou? speak on!

What is it thou wouldst ask of me? a song?

'Tis thine;—or wouldst thou speak of graver

　　　things,

Of wisdom, virtue? though, indeed, to me

Seems nought so grave as song, which has my

　　　soul,

And from a height of heaven o'erlooks the world,

Just as the sun o'erlooks both gay and grave;

But now speak on.

COR.

　　　I have spoken; and cannot add,

As the tone told thee of my speech, I think,

Had I the thousand voices of the sea,

And such an eloquence as might persuade

A god against an oath he has sworn by Styx,

More than the one word of my speech conveys.

Cass. (*coldly*).

I understand thee, and I understood;

But for thine honour's sake hoped that I err'd;

And as one word for question, so one word

Suffices for an answer, and my tone

Is eloquent too, and, sternly as a girl's

Lips can, it speaks the word—Polyxena.

Cor. (*passionately*).

While still the mountain passes, that I cross'd

Before I hither from my princedom came,

Rose betwixt me and Troy, I was betrothed

Because my father will'd; thou wouldst not have

Son disobedient to his sire, a king;

Nor would I be, for fair Polyxena

Is sweet as she is fair ! Nor would I be,

Save for the more than mortal charm that first

Seen here, Cassandra, made my heart its own

As Spring the earth !—Spring hath not less to
strive

With earth, because her victory makes it glad.

CASS.

Deep in the abysses of the ample main,

They say, are sea-flowers, which far, far below

The restlessness, rest always, nor are torn

Up any more when the great rollers raise

Their slippery black hollows fringed with foam,

Than when the sunset streams across the sea

Unbroken from the offing to the shore :

So in my heart, deeper than passion or

The golden moods of calm, has ever bloom'd

My love of innocent Polyxena ;

And, for she has no shame to tell to me

Her secrets, better know I than do you

She loves you.

Cor.

And I guess, part from your speech
And part because the snow of your cymar
Has just the heaving of a summer wave,
That you, my princess, love me! ah, turn, turn
Your eyes upon me, even though more severe
They be than Rhadamanthus's regard.

Cass.

(Nay, there is no heave of my bosom now,
The while I tell thee that I love thee not.
E'en were Polyxena dead—speak not; begone.

[*Exit* Corœbus.

Ah me! ah me! and did my bosom heave?
Polyxena, much I love thee, sister mine,
More than myself! I have spoken a false speech
Which never for mine own sake had I done.
My sister, O my sister! I refute,
Do I not, Paris's philosophy?)

SCENE III.

Priam.

TROJANS! and all whose dwellings are
        betwixt
The pines of Ida and yon purple sea!
The circlet glittering round our royal brows,
The golden orb sway'd by our royal hand,
The robe gem-fasten'd, o'er our royal limbs
That droops its broider'd folds; these things of
        late
Have with their splendour mock'd your monarch's
        mind,
Which restless still, and dark within him moves;
And he knows well that though the clamours go
Up from the plain in honour of his state,
As they were wont when Peace was to the land

Sure as the flowing of Scamander's stream,

Yet that the hearts are restless as the throats.

And now I fear, and know ye with me fear—

Thus, when black cloudlets drifting o'er the sky,

Gather to one great cloud, nor any wind

Dares stir the awful stillness of the air

With e'en a bated breath, men wait the first

Swell of the deepening thunder with more dread

Than when the war in heaven, now at its height,

Flings far its fire and farther rings its peals.

And now—for to his people a king's heart

Should be, I deem, apparent as his crown—

The thing we dread is the bright lady fair

Of Greece—is Helen—whom the flower-wreathed

    prow

Of Paris lately from his Grecian voyage

Returning brought. [*Aside.*] It were not well to

    speak

My mind of him before the people. Would

Some Nereid had dragg'd the losel down,

Seizing his locks, which with aspalathus

He perfumes!—Therefore, people, my resolve

Is that, before the Spartan herald comes,

As come he will unless the war comes first,

We do despatch with escort of a fleet,

And with all speed, back to her palaces

Beside the broad Eurotas, Sparta's queen.—

Do ye applaud? Ye do. I give you thanks.

Enter CASSANDRA.

CASS.

The rush of the birth of the fountains,

    Flash'd bright in the sunlight where

I saw the clouds on the mountains

    As a gauze nigh floating in air;

The eagle,—storms to sheathe him

    In thunder that day were none,

For the towers of Troy beneath him

    Were plain to his eye as the sun.

The peaks and the piny ledges,
   The leap, and the gliding flight
Of the rivers betwixt the edges
   Of mountain and sea, were bright;
And the feet of the gay Hours morris'd,
   Unshod of thunder and rain,
Over mountain and mountain forest,
   Over sea and city-crown'd plain.

The sea with the sun upon it
   Shone afar, and farthest arose
A dazzle that overshone it
   Of high Samothracian snows.
Anigh in the pines was moving
   A wind, neither loud nor drear,
But like to a whisper loving
   Of Zephyr in Oread's ear.

The bee was aloft for the heather,
   I heard the cicada sing,

The warmth of the sunshiny weather
    Made buoyant the moth's weak wing;
And there, not as here they meander,
    But rainbow-arching the fern,
The streams of the sacred Scamander
    Were toss'd from the river god's urn.

And slowly the white clouds drifted,
    And sunshine fathom'd each glen;
But high in her lone haunt lifted
    Far over the cities of men;
The face that pale as a star is
    Of her whom I sought had no smile;
The bride thou hast left, O Paris,
    Forgot not to weep for a while.

Ye who dwell by streams that are wider
    Than where I have seen them to-day,
Would ye know with what gift from Ida
    My footsteps have come away?

From **gold** of the crocus valleys?

   From purple **of** pine-woods high?

From silver of stream **that sallies?**

   Nay; I bring but a prophecy.

The god **A**pollo met **me**

   Where vair was the slope with flowers,

He vow'd that **he would not let me**

   Escape to Ilion's towers;

What he ask'd of me I tell not,

   A maiden pure am I still,

Yet a gift, **though my** girdle fell **not,**

   I won, upon Ida's hill.

O **Ilion** under Ida!

   O listen, **while yet is** pause;—

There draws upon horse and rider,

   Upon breast and babe there draws,

On the lord in his bath who lingers,

   On the slave who speedeth the grist,

On the boy with the lute in his fingers,
    And the girl with the gold round her wrist,—

There draws a more furious thunder
    Than ever did Ilion amaze,
While the width of heaven asunder
    Was never unrent by the blaze;
While, fierce, with the leaping of leopards
    The rivers of Troas came down,
And drifted the sheep and the shepherds
    Nigh over the walls of the town.

But Ida may keep the glory
    Of summer to-day it shows,
Be as blue to its summit hoary
    As the gentian there that blows,
As the skies o'er its head unclouded,
    And Ida's wild bees may hum
Over lawns by no vapour shrouded,
    For not thence shall the darkness come!

Shall come, with no passing crashes

 Of thunder, no transient fears,

But with end that will leave Troy ashes,—

 A tempest of ten long years !

Shall come on her track who has sought us,

 The track that was made, for our sighs,

O'er the sheen of the violet waters,

 By the voyage of the violet eyes !

     [*A general laughter ensues.*

PRIAM.

Trojans ! and strangers harbour'd here in Troy,

Divinity within me works and gives

The lie to this dishevelled prophetess.

Is it with your acclaim that I revoke

Fair Helen's exile which I late decreed ;

For it to her were exile, inasmuch

As Love, the lord of all, is potent o'er

The power that draweth men of fatherland ?

Shall I revoke the sentence? Shall we bear
Ourselves as Trojans, not as timid deer?

ALL.

Ay!

PRIAM.

Your intrepid scorn of this wild girl
Rings to the Rhætian steep—her words are false.

CASS.

In this day of our glory the morning
     Brings over the hills of the east
No task save the task of adorning
     Ourselves for the hours of the feast.
On temples and palaces broken
     The life of the slant ray expires,
And hardly may reach to give token
     To the waves of the west of its fires.

But or roseate as a bride's blushes,
     Or saffron-hued, like to her veil,

The morn over Troas that gushes

    Shall soon be more full on the sail;

No temple or palace shall glister—

    Where Ilion once was there shall be

A ruin burnt out, and a blister

    Of plain betwixt highland and sea.

PRIAM.

Disperse ye with your hearts as careless as

Is youth before life's gray laborious days;

Swung on the wave, a furlong out to sea,

Or emptying his trawl upon the beach,

Beneath the shadow of Sigeum, let

The fisher have no fear except for storm,

Or futile toil; and may his fears be vain!

And where the glens grow narrower, and the

      groves

Higher, until they end, and out of them,

With here and there a pine and mountain ash,

And whitest stripe of torrent, ledge on ledge,

The bulk of Gargarus lessens to a peak

Too steep to keep its snows—there, 'mid the

      growth

That belts the mountain, let the forester

Think of no war but his against the pards.

And let the shepherd by Scamander's stream,

While, like the river, glides the summer's day,

Blue and unaltering in its lapse serene,

Be lull'd to a half-dream, where on the sward

He sits above the reeds, till scarce he knows

Which is, of the two murmurs in his ear,

The river's and which the browsing of his flocks.

And ye who dwell in Troy, let joy be yours

Of heart, and mirth of wine-empurpled lip;

And ye of Troy and Troas, think not of

The future, save of that fast-coming day

Which, with inaugurating litanies

And sacrifice that floods the temple floors,

And hymn that seems to lift the temple roof,

And then with lightfoot dances and the lyre,

And brows bloom-wreath'd, and faces flush'd
    with wine,
That see the morning-star, shall make our hearts
Glad for the bridal of Polyxena;
Look how she blushes! nay, my sweetest child,
The lily is fair enough, nor needs, I think,
To borrow a red petal of the rose.

CASS.

War! war! there is war for Troas
    Shall redden Scamander's reeds,
And Peace,—when the frieze lies low as
    The base, amid rank-growing weeds;
Vain! vain! unheeded, as I am,
    Shall knees be on temple stair;
He lives, who the halls of Priam
    Shall strike with the grating share!

A knife that lifted to fall is
    I see o'er the waves afar;

D

A lingering fleet at Aulis,
 A vision of coming war!
By the gods!—they built our city—
 It may be, it may be yet,
There is hope that gods may pity,
 There is chance that men may forget.

Yes! Greeks will relent if Helen,
 With the joy in her eyes, return,
Or gods will aid if the spell in
 Our hearts of pleasure we spurn:
To the shore! to the shore! O hasten,
 For children, and wives, and sires,
On our throats ere the war-dogs fasten,
 Ere falls our city in fires!

PRIAM.

Prophetic are Cassandra's words, and us
Should gladden and make sure that men shall say
In after time, with envy of our lot:—

" These were the men who lived as peacefully

As now they rest, after the golden days

That went like hours, in Priam's far-off reign."

So shall the speech run of the future time;

For now, by virtue of that sense divine

Which is implanted in a king, I know

That my wild daughter's words, even as are

    dreams,

Are true in this, that their reverse is true.

SCENE IV.

THE CHORUS.

HYMEN! thou lord of blushes,
    And darkness lovelier far
Than light's most lovely flushes
    Around eve's brightening star.

Hymen! be thou propitious
    On this her bridal day,
When joy is avaricious
    Of sweet Polyxena!

Past are the nuptial torches,
    And charr'd, for all to see;
Duly before the porch is
    The jewell'd axle-tree.

Cassandra ! bind thy tresses,
   And flee to hide thy shame,
Up to the hill recesses
   From which thy bodings came !

Out on thee, pale proud virgin,
   Who ne'er knew lover's kiss !
No parcel hath thy dirge in
   A singing like to this !

O the light-footed goddess, who shoots like a
   lance,—
For Hera from heaven moves e'en as we dance,—
We are swift as that huntress whose wont is to
   wear
The moon on her brow and the stars in her hair ;
The roses that wreathe us are red, but seem white,
So rapidly circles the speed of our flight,
But their colour returns when we sudden restrain
Our feet at the swiftest, and sing our refrain—

" O Hymen, O Hymen," and tell our desire

To the unseen god nigh us whom flowers attire

With a crown, and he holdeth a sceptre of fire;

Him each girl of us prays for a veil, and to have

A groom like Coræbus, as comely and brave!

O Hymen! O Hymen! if grace we have found

Let thy marjoram wreath fling a fragrance
          around,

And grant, if a god may by mortals be seen,

One glimpse of the smile on thy loveable mien:

Thou art hid; yet, O sisters, methinks, I per-
          ceive

A more divine scent than of wreaths here we
          weave;

It may be the boding Cassandra prevents

More sign of thy presence than flower-flung
          scents.

Our malison on her! as once she fled, still,

Accurs'd thorough valley, accurs'd over hill,

May she fly, with a fancied Apollo behind,—

That the fairest of gods should in vain have been

    kind !—

May the winds that blow on **her be** ne'er from the

    West !

May her woe by no gladness be ever redress'd !

For she cross'd us **in** peace, and foretold us **of**

    wars,

Of a battle-smoke **soon** that should blot **out our**

    stars !

Like the thunder in summer fear us did affray,

And has pass'd, like **the thunder in summer,**

    away !

The lute, not the trumpet, the scarf, not **the shield,**

The gay banquet-hall, not the red battle-field,

Shall be ours ; and kind **heaven our** peace shall

    prolong

Till the flowing shall end of Scamander **the**

    strong !

No darts, but from **Eros's bow,** shall escape,

No blood flow in **Troy** but the blood **of the grape;**

And, quench'd in long sunshine, the prophecies
    dark
Of Cassandra shall pass e'en from memory ;—
    Hark !

What a tumult's abroad ! to that sudden shout
    listen !
It leaps to the stars high above us that glisten ;
What burden is this that the revellers bear
To join our " O Hymen" that shakes the still
    air ?
Have the youths made a song to Polyxena's
    charms ?
—Aphrodite protect us ! the shout is, " To arms !"
One fleeth this way with the cry on his lips—
" Ho ! what means this panic ?" he answers, " The
    ships !"
And with spear in his hand, and his arm within
    shield,
And greaves but half buckled, he rushes a-field ;

What meant his reply?—O! palsying fear!

The hunt for false Helen is up, and is here;

The seas of our goddess their ships would not

    stay—

Take thy grasp from my garments!—away, girls,

    away!

ACT II. SCENE I.

CASSANDRA.

ENONE!

ŒNONE.

Is it news thou bringest me
From Troy?

CASS.

The Greeks are come.

ŒNONE.

And Helen gone?
Thou answerest not—she stays; stay not with me.

CASS.

At peril from the intercepting Greeks,
Œnone, I have sought thy mountain cave

To tell thee that the unbroken slopes of shale,

Which sheer beneath thee fall, and the rough
　　blocks

Of huger stones than warriors could heave,

And the one ash that flourishes aloft

And whitens with the passing mountain storm,

Here by thy cave, a hardier thing than thou,

May guard thee from wild beasts, but not from
　　men;

And that thou must return with me to Troy:

For, sweet Œnone, know that Ida's slopes

Are free no more to anything, save air;

And with the natural solace comfort thee

That thou art not unfortunate alone;

For ended is at last of Ilion's feast

The long unbroken day, whose summer seem'd

A glory not more transitory than

The songs Apollo makes; but now no more

Upon the pleasant holms at evenfall

The girls and youths link dances; or the girls

O'erload with bloom their flower-baskets, while

The youths, with tenor of their flutes, give forth

A music sweeter than the honey borne

Past them by hiving bees; perfect in vain

The peace of evening falls upon the land:

But betwixt Trojan town and Grecian tent

The ringing battle sways, the chariots charge,

And irresistible Achilles swoops

Like lightning on the forest of our spears.

ŒNONE.

And Paris?

CASS.

Spends the hours upon his hair;

But think not thou art the only hapless one,

Œnone; for Corœbus is or slain

Or captive; he to sudden battle rush'd

Upon his marriage eve, the morn of war.

And our white lily, paler than her wont,

Sits, looking piteously at the stole

He for his armour doff'd :—dost thou regret

The broken bridal of Polyxena?

ŒNONE.

Bid Paris hither come, and I will change

This cavern for another that I know;

'Tis higher up the mountain, and its glen

Sinks, like a mine, into the fir-forest,

Whose broad belt, drawn along the steep hill-side,

Will guard my Paris better than yon towers;

And if the leaguer burst of hostile men

Up the long precipices, and the shout

Ring, where was only sound of breeze or bird,

Since these hard gum-smear'd trunks that are thick

  for miles

Were saplings—still there is shelter—in my arms;

They will not slay a girl; and I will be

Pierced, as is armour, ere his flesh is grazed.

CASS.

Thou thinkest only of thine own cross'd love,

Œnone ; but thine arms thou speakest of,

They are so wasted when I look at them,

From the round pearls of a still recent day ;

I cannot blame thee, we may spare to reprove

The soul, when the heart is broken; . . .on me now

Comes with swift wing my visionary hour;

She asks not why my stature lifts itself,

Why on my limbs is tremor, and in my eyes

Unearthly passion—wild, and yet serene ;—

Nothing she notes, a year might pass before

She raised her downcast face, or stirr'd at all ;

Ah me ! ah me ! the vision of her end

Comes clear from out the mist of future things,

The prophecy is hot upon my lip,

I scarce can stay it.

ŒNONE.

   Do not clasp me thus.—

Thine arms, Cassandra, are not Paris's.

Why is thy gaze as Paris's once was—long ?

CASS.

Wilt thou not follow me down the mountain lawns
To safer shelter than, from beasts and men,
There can be here? thou canst not, for thy limbs
By most exhausting power of hopeless love
Are sapless, as a crone's from wear of years.

ŒNONE.

I would to Troy, but Helen is in Troy.
Bring Paris hither.

CASS.

       Paris—that—well—I will.
Farewell, Œnone, this once let my arms
Hold thee a moment, and my gaze be long,
My playmate of past days, upon thy face,
That in our smiling days smiled more than mine.

SCENE II.

PARIS.

PRITHEE, Cassandra, slower. I have come
Hither. For change. And change, alas, I
have.
The hill is steep; 'tis too precipitous.
My limbs ache; O for rest! for Helen's lap!

CASS.

Hadst thou desired a change, and from the mesh
Of thy Greek courtezan's caressant hair
To disentangle thee, a furlong's space
Was all betwixt her smiles and their red fruit.

PARIS.

But, then, the blood. To see it, heaves my gorge.

Rough are the Greeks; they might have wounded
    me.
This hill's too steep; besides, when one slope's
    climb'd,
Appears another still.   My feet, too, slide,
The shale is slippery.   I will return.

CASS.

Nay, let me to your vanity appeal,
A trifle more of climbing,—you shall have
A triumph such as Hector never won.

PARIS.

You are satirical.   O me, this hill!
And I am shameless.   You offend me not.
Who am not a fool.   But a philosopher.
Do you remember—how this climbing takes
My breath—do you remember, ere I sail'd
For Greece, we talk'd together?   It was then
I prophesied to you the prophetess.

Hinted that though man may have wings, he must

Not fly with them, lest overstrainèd flight

Leave him no power of pinion, e'en so much

As to resist a swift and shameful fall.

And now which in the difference betwixt

Us twain, Cassandra, has the best of it?

I who scorn men, or you who are scorn'd by men;

You who chose love and knowledge, soul and
        mind,

Or I, who neither hate nor love my race,

Who look not in the faces of the Hours

Save for what festal wreaths may hide their brows,

I, to men's praise or blame indifferent?

CASS.

Your feet climb falteringly.   There is no son

Of Priam taller, statelier than you,

Who languish up a slope which girls can climb;

But in the Grecian tents they say is one,

Nireus by name, who is more fair than thou.

PARIS.

Curse on the liars! Cretan speech is truth
Compared to theirs. Fame over all the world
Sows broadcast Paris's name.

CASS.

I think 'tis known
In Lacedæmon, and I would that there,
Whither we climb, it never had been heard.

PARIS.

Nireus! a deeper curse befall him than
Would strike a god for broken Stygian oath;
Nireus, forsooth!

CASS.

My noble brother! moved
Neither by praise nor blame; neither by Troy's
Wounds nor Œnone's broken heart, thy works—

And yet—there is hope for men who vaunt their
     sin ;
Hope will forbear more from the soul of man
Than wife from husband ; and her deadly hate
Comes, or is absent, with Hypocrisy.

Paris.

As for Œnone, I would stake a steed
She has had, or wanted, since I tired of her,
Another fere, as is the wont of girls.
The snow lies low upon this sudden lawn ;
Ha ! 'tis a white stole—something is beneath.

Cass.

Yes ! . . . . .
Death is beneath ; death rigid on the limbs
Which late were youthful with Œnone's life :
And not low skies of morning, leaden hued,
At its hot core, nor pale green lights of eve,

Nor clouds where roseate bloom is even **more**

  brief

Than was her own, nor star-shine **braided heaven,**

Shall reach the eyes o'er **which** [*she stoops*] **I now**

  draw down

The wan lids that have felt so many tears.

Laugh, sing some lilt, Paris, that wears the strings

Of Paphian lutes ; nay, dance, **for to thy feet**

Of climbing there is unexpected end.

Thou spakest truly, Paris, she has sought

And found a new love, and forgotten thee,

In his embrace—in the embrace of Death.

PARIS.

Surprise at this works less with me than thee ;

Hadst thou foreknowledge of her piteous death ?

CASS.

Yes, of the time of it, not of the place ;

Of late, at entrance of her mountain cave,

I stood beside her—me she much besought
To bring thee hither, and while she besought
The knowledge came to me that not again
Œnone's sad voice, and her sadder eyes,
Should meet with mine, till I had welcomed
     Death,
(As much almost as she), and found her where
Eros ne'er was, in a dim quiet land
Beside a stream I covet, Lethe's stream.
And I knew, too, that she should die the first,
And on this mountain, and upon this morn—
That blood upon her stole! it gives the lie,
I think, to what you say of girlish faith.

PARIS.

'Twas cruelty in thee to bring me here.

CASS.

Why?—but I mind me now of what you said,
It is the sight of blood offends your eyes;

Forgive me, I foreknew not that her death

Would other be than thou mightst view unmoved ;

—Nay, I had better hope of thee than this.

And I was kind, not cruel; for I thought

That what nor curses of thy countrymen,

Nor thy sire's anger, nor thy brother's scorn,

Nor any fear that still thou hast of Heaven,

Could bring to pass, with thee, a sight like this

Of poor Œnone dead for love of thee,

Might haply bring to pass; think of the days

When no more ceased thy fond words in her ears

On these high lawns than did the cicale's song ;

And how her feet came eager to meet thine

Over the crocus and the ground ivy : ·

Nor less the crocus and the ground ivy

Now carpet all the sward than then they did ;

And eager o'er them came her feet to-day,

But not so lightly as they came of yore.

Nobler thou wast in those long-perish'd days ;

Looking on this sweet corpse, return to them.

Repentance to Œnone's lover were

More easy than to Helen's paramour.

PARIS.

Let us begone.   Think not I am not moved.

Were I a fool, Cassandra, I should hold

Myself repentant, and make thee elate

At working what not miracles may work :

But this I know, that whatsoe'er, (to take

Your phrase,) I, as Œnone's lover, vow,

I, whom with all men Habit has for slave,

Shall, ere long break, as Helen's paramour.

CASS.

O Paris, Paris, ruin at thy feet

Wrought by thee lies; and far below yon gorge

Where blue Scamander broadens through the

    bowers,

A dim foreknowledge tells me there will soon

Another ruin lie, of Ilion;

And every spear that wounds a Trojan now

Thy hand has flung it, thine has lit the fire

That dimly blazes in my second sight;

And roaring grows and flings out longer arms,

And, to a pyramid soaring, removes Troy,

And sinking when its brief fierce reign is done,

Gives back not what it took, long porticoes,

The busy mart, the palace, where the feast

Sounds from within; the solemn marble shrines—

Up to which the white garments glittering go—

A city splendid, opulent and gay,

In terrace upon terrace rising o'er

The blue plain where' not even may wings reach

    home.

Gives back not this great glory which it took,

But where Troy was, some ashes, and few stones,

And that which shall be to all future time

A wonder, and a pity, and a fame!

I bid thee forth from out the harlot's arms,

Nor less because it is too late to amend
Thy wasted life ; but death is in thy hands,
Nor less is how to die than how to live,
A care to men of honour, therefore, fight
And fall for Ilion that falls for thee.

PARIS.

I will go down to Troy, and leave thee here
To tend Œnone, or what once was she,
And will return with things that may bestow
Some ceremony on her burial.

ACT III. SCENE I.

Chorus.

O we may pass, at last, from out the
    gates,
  The Greeks are gone; ah, bitter as
    the brine
Which lifts them from us, have they made our
    fates,
  And trebly bitter mine.

Say'st thou that pleasure is more sweet for
    pain?
  That, liberated from long leaguer, we
By strong Scamander's banks may dance again,
  And sing and kiss? ah, me!

Man has a heavy lot, but heavier rods
    Smite woman, to the splendour of whose eyes
Youths look, as to the stars look they whose gods
    Are visible in the skies.

Girls' lips, men say, have life and death for them ;
    War in their hearts than love is paler fire :
A lover would, to kiss a garment's hem,
    Forego the crown and lyre ;

But oh ! the serpent in the flowery grass !
    The death that is not parent of the grave !
For to this goddess it must come to pass
    To be scorn'd, as is a slave,

When bloom, which is as Aphrodite's zone,
    Fades, and love's voice is silent in the ears,
Nor life remains, except a monotone
    Of apathetic years.

But I am thrice unblest; what good is it
   To me that pleasures now to Troy return?
I joy in them as those rejoice in wit
   Who are dust within the urn.

What is the song, when it allures not men?
   The dance, unless it wins their eyes, should
      cease;
War may bring death—so it is better, when
   The bloom is past, than peace.

What cares the rose for summer, if the suns
   Belated are, and she is overblown
Ere from the south the spreading warmth fore-runs
   The glorious flying throne?

When hands are idle hearts their work begin;
   Peace now is ours, alas! for me too late,
Whose girlhood went while panic was within,
   And strife without the gate.

My feet forget the dance—'tis ten years since
    They plied it, when Polyexna was wed;
E'en now, 'tis said, to our rescue by her prince
    Mygdonian troops are led—

Not needed—though, indeed, if the last lie
    Of raven-soul'd Cassandra should be true,
And Greece come back with fire, what care I
    Whose rose is turn'd to rue?

SCENE II.

CASSANDRA *at the shrine of* APOLLO.

CASSANDRA.

STILL on the far verge of the eastward plain
   Gathers no dust; Coræbus, thy escape
From long captivity was vain for us,
For still thou comest not; and now is built
Up to its highest step yon altar where
Polyxena must perish. I would give,
To see the dawn of thy far-flashing spears,
My hope of early death. But yestereve
Thy succour would have seem'd superfluous,
A mere bravado to the beaten Greeks,
At last, forsooth, departing;—'twere to-day
As useless, for the intervening night
Of fury and alarm, of fire and sword,
Sets morn for ever far from Ilion!

How splendid shone the city yesterday,

As though triumphant, and all Troas laugh'd

In sunlight!—Ida of the many peaks,

The terraced town, the champaign, and the shore

Where Greece seem'd gathering to her distant

     ships.

Our citizens were out upon the plain,

And, after ten wild years, our rivers were,

With their cool streams and shades, our friends

     again,

And, all her tears gone, Polyxena,

Expectant of Corœbus, look'd adown

The garlanded gay street—and now the knife

Is almost at her throat! not even Greeks,

Surely, would more than threaten such a deed,—

Whose end is not of those that I fore-know.

Enough, that Trojans are all slain or ta'en,

And their rejoicing Troy a ruin charr'd

By stratagem, and a more fatal night

Than that which gave the Danaids revenge.

I think 'tis pity this base stratagem,

Bloody as base, should not have fail'd to end

This memorable siege where Victory

So long poised doubtfully her eagle wings

O'er valour great and patient on both sides,

As his, the mighty hero's, whose sad eyes,

Strain'd over Calpe, swept the western wave

For those blest isles where flowers blow, but no
> wind.

And—ha!—below there—on the plain—the shout!

The press—it hides the altar—is she there?

O hand uplifted falter,
> O priest with the knife forbear;
O ye gods—is she laid on the altar?
> Is it bloody, her soft brown hair?
> > > *[She kneels.*

God of the bow that errs not! Giver of death!

Monarch of light, and master of the lyre!

Without whom all the beauty of the earth,

Save for dim Dian and her dimmer stars,

Were dark as the dread realms that own thee not;

With whom that earth is glory, spreading 'neath

Thy beamy throne hues, golden, red, and vair

Of flowers, and green of groves, and blue of hills,

Save of their windy summits, when alight

Thine amethystine sandals! Power! to whom,

Besides the lordship of the visible light,

Belongs the illumination of the soul;

Without whom man is blind in spirit, and base,

With whom, from dwarf deform'd, sullen, and

        harsh,

His soul grows to a giant, gracious, pure,

And nobly scornful, with a front as nigh

To heaven as that lone Titan's, who bears up

For ever the pale burden of the stars :

God! who didst loosen once the laurel wreath

About thy brows with turmoil of the chase,

O'er Ida after me, Cassandra, here

Thy suppliant; O let this memory sway

Thee, as, in men, thou swayest memory!

O think how thy communicated breath

That is life and love and blessing otherwhere,

To me came with a curse, and blasted me

For ever from the nature of a girl,

And do me some amends; spare, king, O spare!

By thy deep eyes, and ample uplift brow,

Spurn thy revenge, and spare Polyxena!

I will look forth from where the parapet

Is half burnt down, and ragged from the flames:

Far down below me is the plain; on it,

Betwixt what seem two threads as motionless

And blue as a steel helmet-rim, and are

Simois and great Scamander; on the space

Whose level stretches broad betwixt these streams

I see the multitude sway to and fro

Of cruel Greeks, and hidden by their press

Stands the high altar, and I mark the advance

Towards it of those who lead Polyxena ;

For whom the crowd parts upon either side,

And closes up again. O that fierce, hoarse cry,

Bloodthirsty from a myriad of throats !

In Ilion's happy day that is no more,

Not such the murmur which through breathless
    air

Arose to priestesses, their rites perform'd,

Who look'd down hence—but sound of shrilly
    flutes

And laughter distance-temper'd—and the shout

Of those who hurl'd the quoit, or, joyously

Tried the mock skirmish with their blunted spears.

The murmur grows, 'tis edged now with alarm,

They press out eastwards now—those are not
    Greeks

That meet them, as though a sudden sea should
    roll

To meet the long Ægean shoreward swell

With a roar, and a flinging far of foam, as of spears;

The murmur rises now to wild and shrill,

The plain is all in tumult—O for this

Bright hope of rescue, I pour thanksgiving.

Apollo—yes, the battle cry sounds up—

Apollo—thanks to thee—Coræbus comes!

SCENE III.

Paris.

SINCE from the flame-lit tumult of the night

    I fled into this cellar and there crouch'd,

Forth-looking but to hear of the defeat

Of some tumultuous rescue—since the night,

This phial of hemlock juice a score of times

Has risen to my lips, and been withdrawn

A score of times, save one; suppose once more

I argue with myself—I have leisure now,

And something need to while away the time;

For even if in this dark and dismal place

Some one had left a lute, I durst not sweep

Its strings, lest on me I should draw the Greeks.

Now, let me see, if I kill not myself

The Greeks will kill me, or they, at the least,

Will make a slave of me, and lop my hair;

The most might very like be more than death

That they would do. I had best be brave and drink.

I shall be more esteem'd in Tartarus,

And be there sooner but by half an hour;

And even though the gibber of some ghosts

Shall quaver round me angrily, yet one

Will have soft words, and whatsoe'er a ghost

May show of love and kindness; I shall feel

Œnone's shadowy arms around my shade.

I fear one's life will be monotonous;

But upon Charon I may put some jests

And flirt a little with Persephone.

Ten minutes more, for ordering my hair

Before this pocket mirror—I am pale.

This ringlet is too dry—its twist wants oil—

The hemlock juice will moisten it—so—the rest

I—courage, Paris—drink—and wait for death.

SCENE IV.

CASSANDRA.

FAR-DARTER, though thine ear be hitherto
   Rejectant of my prayers, yet once again
My knees are bent, my hands are raised to thee.
If aught thou hast of pity; if thou art
Less marble than thy statues, grant this prayer.
Choose from thy shoulder-shaken quiver out
The keenest pointed, truest-feather'd shaft,
And shoot it through this heart of mine, that I
May in the same hour with Polyxena
Reach the dim shore, where we shall find the sad
Œnone, playmate of our happy youth.

Where, if the wave be sullen, and the land

Arid and dark, nor ever any voice,

Save shrill weak wailing sometimes of a ghost

Challenge the silent victory of night;

Yet, if may be we drink of Lethe's stream,

There are no memories of lost joy and pride;

And, certes, red-hand slaughter is not there,

Nor scorn for prophecies that are but too true,

Nor love suppress'd in hearts that therefore break.

Enter CORÆBUS, *wounded.*

COR.

Cassandra !

CASS.

Thou here with thy routed troops?

Fly—stay—thou—

COR.

Didst thou speak of love suppress'd?

CASS.

Thou art wounded.   Let me stanch it with my
    robe.

COR.

I am wounded to the death by a chance spear,
Yet the lost battle have I left to find
Thee, and have found thee.   Hear my last few
    words,
Cassandra, and support me with thine arm,
And hold thy raiment tighter to my heart;—
I play'd, I think, the honourable man
To sweet Polyxena, whose life, with mine
'Tis like, is bleeding now away; but hear
The last words that I speak, which through my
    life
All speeches of my heart had for refrain.
Thou, thou, Cassandra wast, and art, my love,
And shalt be if love lives in phantom-land;
If thou, Cassandra, couldst declare that thou

Hadst love for me, suppress'd, as late I heard,

My end upon this earth were easier than

The end of those here, who, as fable runs,

Or truth, I know not, pass'd from this dull sphere

To the high feast of gods, nor yet knew death.

Cass.

Yes, I may speak; lean lower thy dear head—

Move not thy lips—thine eyes, alas, seem not

To know me, but thine ears can drink my

    words.

I loved thee ever—nor was my love the less

Because it was despair; and I have felt

'Twas this that made Apollo's passion vain.

Lift not thy lips, I will stoop mine own...... This

    kiss,

Ah me! is younger than my lover's death.

A maiden's love is ever a soft thing,—

I am strangely gentle in my mood, nor mad,

Nor sad above his corpse. Hark! from the plain

Leaps one great shout, as high as Ida's peak,

And all the gathering of the people parts,

And I can just perceive the altar's pile;

O ye great gods! if vengeance is in Heaven

For barbarous deed of hell, let it o'erwhelm

That coward shout; it greets my sister's blood;

Red is that altar now, and all my tears,

Which my soft sorrow for Coræbus had,

Are turn'd to fire now for Polyxena.

Enter GREEKS.

FIRST GREEK.

Princess, we are sent by Agamemnon's lips

To bear thee to his tent.

CASS.

This sword I snatch

From my dead lover's side is my reply—

Until I have cursed you with the bitterest lips

That hate, and fury, and contempt, can writhe.

FIRST GREEK.

We had best wait till Agamemnon comes,
For the wild prophetess is very fair;
Look how her noble stature and high brow
Front us, on these the loftiest temple steps
Of Troy, o'erlooking the charr'd terraces,
And the wide champaign to its fringe of sea,
And blue length of the streams, and e'en the slopes
Where first they rise of Ida far away.
She waves her wild white arms—the wrath is pale
Upon her mouth—she pours her prophecy.

CASS.

Go back, with more contumely laden
    Than ever were slaves, to your lord;
Tell him this—Greeks can murder a maiden,
    But not if she brandish a sword;
At last your revenge may content ye,
    O well is your victory won!
Of our men slain by night you repent ye—
    And slaughter our maids in the sun!

The hissing of spear-shafts is over,
   No sweat now nor blood is outpour'd,
Sad silence is falling to cover
   The space where the red battle roar'd;
Struck are tents, and your sails ye are setting,
   And Troy where the mirth was, shall soon,
And for ever, all sounds be forgetting,
   Save jackal's howl under the moon.

And Greece shall rejoice in her glory;
   There children shall cease from their play,
Hearts burn under heads that are hoary,
   E'en lovers their whispering stay,
To hear, while the hours fleet unheeded
   By charm of the rhapsodist's strain,
How the gods the just vengeance impeded,
   Of Greece upon Troy, and in vain.

Yet it shall be that Greece shall a guerdon
   E'en greater of glory enjoy;

She shall lay on Fame's pinions the burden
    Of Salamis rather than Troy:
She has sat for ten years in pavilions,
    Ere levell'd were one city's towers;
But the might of the Orient's millions
    Shall be laid by her low in ten hours.

Nor her fame shall be only of valour,
    Whose voice, like a fierce clash of arms,
Shall over the East spread a pallor,
    And over the West stir alarms.
Her arts shall command the world's wonder,
    And the star of her arms shall be down,
When there lives in men's ears, like a thunder
    Of music, the gentler renown.

She shall build, and her structures in ruin,
    Than others that stand be more fair;
She shall carve, and for ever be new in
    Men's souls, to the sculptor's despair.

She shall paint, and when canvas and colour
    Are lost by Time's fury and fret,
All pictures to men shall seem duller
    Than her's which are but a regret.

Her words shall be fire in all ages,
    Wherever the tyrant's abhorr'd;
The life shall not fail of her sages
    Wherever the fool is not lord.
The uttermost reach of Time's river
    Shall end, ere her epic's flight tire,
With echo that waxes for ever,
    Her hand shall be loud on the lyre.

The names of her nymph-hiding fountains,
    And muse-haunted hills shall be known
To men through all time as the mountains
    And streams of the land that they own;
The souls shall her fulness inherit,
    Of statesmen, and sage, and those whom

The beauty and blight of the spirit
    Have gifted with glory and gloom.

Yes ! Greece shall have empire outlasting
    The kingdoms of earth that shall be
On the long lapse of Time, as the wasting
    Of foam on a turbulent sea :
The crown set her starry eyes over
    No rude hands of change shall unbind,
For its realm, which the skies fail to cover,
    And night to conceal, is the mind !

FIRST GREEK.

All know Cassandra's blessing is a bale,
Some dread mishap is boded to our land.

CASS.

But think ye that Ilion's daughter,
    To bless, not to curse ye, here stands?
Her lover's, her sister's late slaughter,
    Ye cravens, yet drips from your hands !

Intent to my words ye have hearken'd,

  Now hear of your country's long shame ;

The cloud by the sun is but darken'd,

  And disgrace shall be blacker for fame.

A dull, bitter herb is the sorrel,

  In Troy turn'd to fields it shall grow,

And greenly the conquering laurel

  On Greece's proud forehead shall show ;

But a time there shall be of despising

  The strength that made Ilion to cease,

When the sun shall be weary of rising

  On deeper dishonours of Greece.

Greece ! Wisdom and Valour shall put her

  High over the nations of earth ;

But to fall, nor have spirit to mutter

  A curse on the hour of her birth ;

At the base of the throne she once sat on

  She shall be as a footstool—and there

G

She shall grovel, and fawn, and be spat on,
  And, out of her meanness, forbear.

The swords that are offer'd to do her
  Their service, she faintly shall aid,
The cowardice still shall cling to her
  That butcher'd yon yet bleeding maid.
Her sons but to lies in the city,
  And theft on the seas, shall be born,
When her past shall draw tears forth of pity,
  Her present shall freeze them to scorn.

Is victory reft from the **Dardan** ?
  That vengeance of scorn still remains;
Misfortune like *ours* may have pardon,
  We shall not be content to be slaves.
But Greece, the world's mightiest nation,
  Shall yet be its meanest, and cower,
As base in her long degradation
  As fierce in her conquering hour.

Nor men only shall not avail her :—
   When fortune's clear shining is done,
When Time's gather'd tempests assail her,
   Her gods shall fall, each from his throne;
Her gods, by whose power we have perish'd,
   Who brought Helen safe o'er the sea ;
Who slaughter'd my sister most cherish'd,
   And poison'd the gift they gave me.

Yes! Jove, the great god and gross lover,
   And Pallas, and Pan, and the rest,
Like so many Vulcans flung over,
   Shall fade to a fable and jest;
The gods as their Greeks would I banish,
   Would spoil them of victim and priest;
And the one I should grieve to see vanish
   The most, men would mourn for the least.

First Greek.

Her ecstasy grows languid, and the breath
Of fierce false inspiration fades in her.

CASS.

That one is, O false, fair Apollo,

    Most heavenly traitor! not thou,

Who vainly Cassandra didst follow

    With Daphne's death green on thy brow.

'Tis the god who is lord of pale Hades,

    Where all things, save quietness, cease ;

I would fain be assured where, when fade his

    Dim meadows and streams, may be peace.

FIRST GREEK.

Princess, we, listening, learn that our fair land

Shall always prosper, and our holy gods

Who have given us victory always in return,

Have honour from our honourable vows.

But lo! thy master, Agamemnon, comes,

I see his plumes where they had yesterday

Bent, ere the fire left of yon arch but shafts.

MISCELLANEOUS POEMS.

TIED TO THE TOWN.

SUMMER, swaying thy sceptre over
 Sea quiet as hill, hill blue as sea,
Thou hast love for all things except thy
 lover,
O Summer, my love, I am mock'd of thee.
I would be near thee, I would be risen
 From the blinding world-wave that beats me
  down;
But, alas! thy throne is not near my prison,
 For I am tied to the flowerless town.

What is it to me that men say she reigneth,
 The glorious Summer, everywhere;

This Summer, who rules the town, attaineth
 But in name to be like my mistress fair.
My love had flowers in her golden tresses,
 And I heard her voice where the brooks
  descend ;
And she stepp'd o'er the green hill-wildernesses,
 And stopp'd in the vales, where the faint ways
  end.

And I know that my queen for a brief, bright
 season,
 Beyond my amorous sight now stands,
Giving, while stay'd is the thunder's treason,
 Fires from her eyes and flowers from her hands.
She has worship enough—it does not grieve her
 That my lips may not to her robe be drawn,—
The sun for the love of her will not leave her,
 For his last light dies not before his dawn.

Her joy over earth like a song is ringing,
 The clouds are as pearls for her, strung in air ;

Scarce at her feet is the blue wave swinging,
　　And the wind will not lift her warm gold hair.
O lovely Summer! as Palamon, longing,
　　When his love was nigh, at her feet to be,
With the dungeon bars his desire still wronging,
　　So yearn I, love of my soul, for thee.

O queen who makest of earth a garden,
　　Thy realms thou losest, but never thy throne;
By the sweetness of thy smile, a pardon
　　For the world he hates from Time is won ;
Till the days when thy rich imperial charm is
　　No longer only to me denied ;
When the lags of the flight of the flower armies
　　Are crush'd by the conquering Winter's stride.

O Summer! Summer! my love thou knowest,
　　It was born with my youth, O grant me one
Of the long rich smiles before thou goest,
　　Thou givest thy lover the lingering sun.

O ! because I love in less fading fashion

   Than he—at thy bright feet let me cleanse

My soul with wells of divinest passion,

   Ere the grey gorse turneth to gold in the glens.

ON CALPE.

A SKETCH.

HE pauses: now to him no more still seems
    Sky nearer, and sea farther, but the lands
Are all beneath him; skimm'd by sunset, gleams
    The ocean of his search; gazing, he stands.

Sun-splendours jewelling an ampler breast
    Of sea than he has seen; no sail, no soil,
Water, and wind, and wings—this was the West,
    This the reward of pioneering toil.

Yet a more sweet reward to hero than
    Far o'er the surges if that long seaboard
Had reach'd his gaze, to prophesy how man
    Should of the West, as of the East, be lord.

Of which he deem'd not—rather to the sun,

    The fellow traveller of his westering way,

With envy look'd, wishing he too might shun

    Men, by the breadth of the Atlantic spray.

Not all ill-starr'd, for though fate him compell'd

    'Mid men to work, and not have life's desire,

Solace he found in scorn of things withheld,

    Friendship and love, wine, leisure, and the lyre.

Loathing he had for trivial human things,

    As of the monsters he must still subdue;

Less sad than was the wisest of earth's kings,

    To look on the world's rose, and name it rue.

Not his the Ithacan's deep-studied part

    To wander everywhere, and all to please;

With an unrest more noble at his heart,

    Beyond the haunts of men, came Hercules.

Restless and tameless as the lion, whose
  Spoil his broad shoulders bare, he saw man-
    kind,
And knew them, and by knowledge did not lose
  The melancholy of the greater mind.

Men's earth, he deem'd, was ended with this
    shore,
  So yearn'd to stand and watch where only sky
Rose from a water-world, that ne'er upbore
  The dust Death spurns with heel of victory.

But if that sunset-silent West had given
  A wind forth, prophesying there should live
Beyond those waves where yet no ship had
    striven,
  The life from which he now was fugitive—

Vainly he had climb'd Calpe to forget
  Care on its rock ; but, failing to divine

O'er the illimitable violet,
    Aught of mankind, he found his anodyne.

*   *   *   •   **

From such a rock, o'er the same ocean range,
    Long after Hercules, Napoleon
Thus watch'd the sunset, wondering no change
    Show'd of the orb on Austerlitz that shone.

One rid the world of monsters, one of men;
    Earth is betwixt them on their thrones of fame;
I think, could Hercules be umpire, then
    Their merit were less different than the same.

But now brow was not knit, nor lips were stern,
    He dropp'd his club, forgot his latest scars,
Gazing, while Heaven pour'd from its deep blue
        urn,
    First flowers—the sunset, and then gems—the
        stars.

Yet somewhere set in the Atlantic seas,

    Those islands of the Blest still fail'd his ken,

Where was desire to roving Hercules

    To rest, with heroes—not with gods, or men.

At last the hero down the steep that burn'd

    No more (for the sun's bow was now unbent),

From wondering at the silent West, return'd

    To wearying of the loud Orient.

Not knowing, to the champaign as he drew,

    How those twin rocks were rent to his renown,

But ill-content, while twilight dropp'd, and dew,

    Upon the pale leaves of his poplar crown.

THE RECTOR'S APOLOGY.

I'M bless'd with a fair benefice, the living may
    be worth
Five hundred pounds a year, at most; east, west,
    or south, or north,
Where'er it is, it matters not, if you try you won't
    divine,
For there's many a country rector in a plight
    resembling mine.

Though what I'm going to tell of might make
    a bishop swear,
I've hitherto borne patiently Life's load of cark
    and care;

But when my *Punch* * turn'd on me, who was
    wont that care to while,
'Twas a case of *Et tu, Brute,* and it fairly roused
    my bile.

You say I starve my curate, that I put, without
    remorse,
His precious life in danger, and work him like
    a horse,
While I play the magnifico—you go a deal too
    far,
You little know, thrice happy *Punch,* what curates
    really are.

A cottage *not* in ruins, and ninety pounds a
    year,
A pittance, as you'd call it, I suppose, I give him
    clear;

---

* These verses were first published in *Punch.*

H

I can't afford to offer more, and still perform
      the feat,
With wife and growing family, of making both
      ends meet.   .

A gentlemanly curate who shows, without pre-
      tence,
That white ties are compatible with charity and
      sense,
Is rare as bird of Paradise; I scatter sans
      avail,—
For like it, he alights not—the salt for such a
      tail.

The lion in the pulpit, and out of it the dove,
I mean the Evangelical, whom all old ladies love,
The slap-you-on-the-back sort, that are muscular
      and " broad,"
The hectic-flush'd who fast, and wear a miniature
      of Laud :

Yes, all I have found wanting, e'en, brought up
    from a child
By careful aunts, the primly good and sentimental-
    mild,
The Calvinist who damn'd us all one week, and,
    which perplex'd
Our minds, the neologian who saved us all the
    next.

A saint who carped at marriage, and preaching,
    flung the pearls
To swine, if swine could take the form of pretty
    English girls;
To have *one* wife, he said, was sin; not so the next
    man, who
Made up, I very soon found out, for him, by
    having two.

Another—scarce it edifies such curate freaks to
    show,
Short, thick, and oleaginous, opinions very low;

He from Dissent converted, and, which scarce so
    well I took,
Then married,—within six weeks from the day he
    came,—my cook.

Next week the place is vacant; it often is; there
    lies
The note of the sole applicant e'en now before my
    eyes;
" Do I object to waltzing, some idiots do, if so,
What points at the whist parties, and is the
    croquet slow?"

Well, *Punch,* old boy, you've 'sulted me, as once,
    becoming " tight,"
My curate to the bishop said, and challenged him
    to fight;
But vengeance, save a single wish, I'll lay upon
    the shelf,
I only wish that you, *Punch,* were a rector like
    myself.

THIRLMERE.

BENEATH the huge Helvellyn
   A lake lies, long and fair,
Which, slenderly outswelling,
   With any may compare;
Here widening and there narrow,
   Like neck and breast of swan,
That soar'd for Dunmail's barrow
   In elfin age agone;
But from the far north flying
   Sank on tired pinion here,
And, with a wild song dying,
   Was changed into a mere.

THE NIGHTINGALE.

IF thy notes, brown bird, over ocean heard
 Could reach her shell-pink ear,
They would seem to her sweet, but ah, more sweet
 My vows to her seem'd last year;
O nightingale, thy power now prove,
 Yet thy best will in vain be sung;
If it challenge her share in the speech of a love
 That is dead now, and should be young.

That is no more on at least one shore
 Of the sea which apart us drave;
Yes! dead and buried, without, may be,
 So much as a stone by its grave;
Yet, if our love be a toy which away
 You on the one shore throw,
I, proud and glad of my agony, say
 On the other it is not so.

She has a memory, hardly that,
　My hope of her is as good;
She has trod on my heart, and its wine in the vat
　Of her victims is redder than blood;
Her eyes now are soften'd for other feres,
　Her laughter rings light and free,
While I am alone, and the bitterest tears
　Would seem mirth were they shed by me.

" Love is the flower of life," I said;
　And kiss'd you, that mouth of yours,
From others, as once from me, its red
　Now averts yet kisses endures:—
Some one kisses you now ! it is well for us all
　That the sea betwixt us roars,
Or, dying, not wooing, he should fall
　At the light-o'-love feet he adores !

And I am a Christian man, forsooth,
　Yes ! and better Christian than those

Who only for want of depth and truth
    Are quick to forgive their foes;
To foil the tempter I think God sets
    The broad blue bar of the main
'Twixt me and the land where my love forgets
    When she prays, to pray for my pain.

Girl! I hate you in spite of your spell;—
    We abide at the earth's extremes,
And I cannot reach to kill you,—well,
    I can kiss you—in my dreams;
O those eves we stood on the moonlit sward!
    If for them who on earth have striven
It be hard to lose it—how much more hard
    To have found, and then lost, heaven!

My dear, my darling,—yet I will come
    Though apart wild waves us rend,
Fitly the restless sea were my home,
    The passionate storm my friend:

I will come, though since she was mine, a score
    Of lovers have sipp'd her charms,
I will kneel and forget to forgive, if once more
    My love will lie in my arms.

Be still, wild heart! be my anger allay'd,
    She is e'en like the rest of them;
To a baser than Cophetua's maid
    I added a diadem.
But for pride, to follow her were not amiss,
    For, although we met last year,
She has since forgot my face, and a kiss
    That is strange, would, to her, be dear.

No! I will stay, and friends shall give
    Few tears and many smiles;
" Wait," they say, " Time's strength will rebuild
      at length
    The ruin wrought by her wiles.

When the years," they tell me, " from youth
    detach
  You far, you may meet perchance,
And lightly talk while you sit to watch
  Her son and your daughter dance."

Yes, forsooth, she will see me and turn a third
  Of her mind from match-making;
And, as if I had never won fonder word,
  She, while ring of the dance follows ring,
Will give me her hand and I shall bend,
  And with smiling indifference say,
" I am glad to see so fair a friend
  Has found back hither her way."

Nay, never, O never shall this thing be !
  The world may forget its wars,
The moon to draw the amorous sea,
  The sun to light the stars ;

If despair for the times when her heart lay on
    mine,
  For the minutes with kisses rife,
For the hours when I drank her eyes as wine,
  Can cease to darken my life.

Yes! I forget not the days that drew
  Up the world to empyreal height,
That banish'd the thunder, and overthrew
  The great black towers of the night;
Should the norland wind be but bitter in frost
  When his love, the Summer, is gone,
And the winds of the earth's end uttermost,
  Her flower-kisses have won?

If the years that sever from youth and give
  Less than they take away,
Would teach me like others forgetful to live
  Of the love I told Heaven was for aye;

Let an early death be mine, and a grave

   Where she shamed the nightingale's tongue,

And let the stone this epitaph have,

   " Whom the gods love die young."

ICHABOD.

(Written, June, 1868.)

" SOMETHING too much of this"—of
struggle, lest
Too slowly Life its soaring wings should ply;
I hope that, after Death, I may find rest,
And have a little, too, before I die.

" *Væ victis*," thunder'd the barbarian,
" Only the vanquish'd grieve."   I think not
thus;
I with an envious gaze the vanquish'd scan,
I, who am one of the victorious.

I, with " *en avant*" ringing in my ears,
I, on whose fatherland the Future smiles,

Here where the favour of the fickle years
 Still is as sunrise o'er the Queen of Isles.

I, in my mood, turn from the masts that start
 Like forests up from English estuaries,
—Turn from the gold on every busy mart
 Falling in richer shower than Danae's.

From press and turmoil of the eager throng,
 Shaking the ladder up whose rungs they strive,
From prosperous summer, ringing loud and long,
 With busy buzzings of the giant hive.

From voices than this tumult nobler far,
 From poet proffering me still his flowers,
From sages who, no lower than the star
 Bid me to look, shouting from rival towers.

From this I turn, perplex'd, and blind, and deaf,
 To where the Present has subdued its strain,

To where Life is as Death—to where the sheaf
  Is housed, and idle are Time's hands—to
    Spain !

Land of the river of the golden sands !
  Thy glories, like that gold, but fable seem ;
Past is the sceptre from thy sunburnt hands,
  Lost from thy dark eyes their imperial gleam !

Land whence went forth, the one like lightning
    hurl'd,
  The other free as wind upon the seas,
The soldier and the sailor of the world,
  The Carthaginian and the Genoese !

Where the swart Spaniard to the swarthier Moor
  Brook'd not to yield on many a battle plain ;
Gone is the Paynim—does his rival, o'er
  Ocean and earth who domineer'd, remain ?

Land opulent in fable, echoing aye
    The horn that sounded through wild Ronces-
        valles!
Where still the strength of Hercules its way
    Seemeth to cleave through Calpe's high sea-
        wall!

Land of Cervantes! who right fitly seems
    Thy jester with his melancholy mirth;—
Land sainted still with what Murillo's dreams
    Drew down from heaven and lifted up from
        earth!

It is not that thou livest, and hast lost
    The nature and the art that made thee fair;—
The flower still of thy year knows never frost,
    Still fragrance steeps thy Andalusian air.

Thy Seville, Venus of earth's cities, yet
    Rises from out her sea of golden bowers;

Still, when in heaven the red and blue are met,
   Glitters Toledo of the hundred towers.

The sweetness is not taken with thy breath,
   Thy golden forests yet link sea and sea,
As with some beauteous queen, laid out in death,
   Wearing her splendours, so it is with thee.

Thy ships still sail, thy grapes grow, in the sun,
   Purple, as still is waved thy daughters' hair;
Thy muleteers sing, thy dances are not done :—
   But life has hope, and thou hast but despair.

Yet, as when a man's dust is dropp'd down deep,
   And cover'd, somewhat sorrow is redress'd,
To think, as our eyes follow, that in sleep
   Which wakes not with earth's morn, there may
     be rest.

So might one muse, and listening to the war

    Of winds on that Sierra where Spain's kings

Lie, would betwixt Granada and Navarre

    See but the shadow the Escurial flings.

ELTER WATER.

THE light clouds drift above thee,
   The woods, as if they love thee,
     Are whispering around;
The Greek who there had sought her,
Had found in Elter Water
     The Naiad, lily-crown'd.

The white and happy village!
The slopes of flowery pillage
     For bees, the stream and isles !—
I think the lake is fairest
When tempest-rain is rarest,
     When Summer is all smiles.

But when the mists veil Nature,
And seems the mountain stature,
     Above thee towering, higher;

I, with a lover's duty,

Thy passionate dark beauty,

Still gaze on, and admire.

Yet wish the mist-sent blindness

May leave my sight, and kindness

To thy fair face return;

O! to thy eyes, my Naiad,

Heaven's lapis lazuli add,

And smiling hold thy urn.

THE BULL AT BALA.

THE peak of Arran on the left!
 Hard on the right the rocks shoot down
To where, along their side, is cleft
 The mountain road to Bala town.

The road o'erhangs the vale and falls,
 By many a wild and winding way,
To vast and various view that palls
 Not through the lapse of Summer's day.

The billowy mountains blue afar!
 Some giant sculptor's fancy warm,
You'd think, had watch'd the ocean's war,
 And carved the statue of a storm.

The lake of Bala, and the rills
    That in it lose their mountain glee,
And westward, towering o'er the hills,
    The throne whence Idris sees the sea!

A glorious scene you might mistake
    For Paradise!—its Eve was there;
Than garden rose glass'd in the lake,
    Than hyacinth on the hills, more fair.

The Bull at Bala was her home,
    She made appear, behind the bar,
The porter's froth as nectar's foam,
    And flavour'd e'en the cheap cigar.

Nor did I, gazing, wonder much
    That hers was still a maiden's grace,
She seem'd a radiant Hebe, such
    Would choose no mate of mortal race.

The rustic Welshman, amorous,
    Drank hard, his spirit high to strain,
And often dared, encouraged thus,
    To vow, but ever vow'd in vain.

" Her eyes but useless arrows shoot;
    She seeks," said Malice, "to ensnare
Some youth of light preposterous suit,
    Short pipe, and all the tourist air."

But these, they flung their knapsacks down,
    And stay'd to flirt an hour or so,
Then pass'd away from Bala town,
    Like winds that kiss the rose and go.

    *   *   *   *   *

I came and went, a year rolled round,
    I, wandering down that vale once more,
Took at the Bull mine ease, but found
    No lovely barmaid as of yore.

I ask'd the waiter, " Is she wed,
    This girl for whom e'en gods might pine ?"
" She married, sir," the waiter said,
    " A gent in the commercial line."

      *   *   *   *   *

I heard,—my eye in London soon
    Gave contradiction to my ear;
For I one summer afternoon
    Down Rotten Row my steps did steer.

Tired I sat down, and ever on
    Flow'd past me Fashion's rising tide,
Until a whisper fell upon
    Me musing, murmur'd down the Ride.

" 'Tis she,"—I look'd, a sudden thrill !
    The place, the time, appear'd a dream;
Back flash'd the climbing of the hill,
    The fishing, futile, in the stream.

For here, the while her fair cheek glow'd,
  Such gaze from that gay throng to win,
A Duke beside her bridle—rode
  The lowly maid of Bala's inn.

Both low and high, and near and far,
  This duke had sought, without avail,
A duchess ; yet star after star
  Drew ducal sunshine but to pale.

He long'd than languid city maid
  To pluck some blossom freshlier blown,
But found the girls of glen and glade
  Knew nought of life beyond their own.

At last, in bagsman's guise and gig,
  The eccentric noble drove away ;
He took the name of Mr. Higg,
  And spent in search a year and day.

Until in Bala's town, a place

    Wild, yet where tourists' wheels are whirl'd,

He found a bride of rural grace,

    Combined with knowledge of the world.

VIOLET.

" NAY, Violet, 'twere foolish freak
　　To change thy name, ma belle,
Which, when its music sweet I speak,
　　Doth aye my thraldom tell
To the dark eyes and pearly cheek
　　That fit that name so well."

She answer'd very wearily:—
　　All round, in sunset-swoon,
Lay richly tranced, as on the sea
　　Sank the last sun of June,
Bequeathing to each orange-tree
　　Rathe relics of his noon.

" My name," she said, " I would forget,
   Alas ! I grew as grows
The flower which is my namesake, yet
   The last heaven's dew to lose ;
The dew best loves the *violet :*
   The rifler bee the *rose :*

" Ah me ! the rover lingereth,
   Yet, well I know, anon
Comes hint of some new odorous breath
   The west wind's wings upon,
And leaves me to a lonely death
   Ere many suns have shone."

Past her, with step which is a dance,
   The southern summer reels ;
Right through the heart of her romance
   Death's darkling stroke she feels,
And turns despair to dalliance,
   Nor, save for kisses, kneels.

" Oh clasp me closer, murmuring
   ' My Rose;' like fiery wine
I drink thy love, while, vanishing
   Down vistas of the vine,
Fades the pure floweret of the spring,
   Whose name no more be mine !"

THE HEBRIDES.

I AM smitten, I am smitten, and the song
    Is dumb upon my lips,
Nor can soar upon a pinion strong
    To the clouds, above the ships;
It is daunted, as a halcyon here might be,
Although upon a tranquil sea;
It is daunted, where the Summer faintly smiles,
Drops few flowers in the depth of the defiles,
While the hills forget the wind, and the sea for-
    gives the Isles.

Towards the sea from as barren hills I gaze,
    And an awe my spirit takes:
With what power weak man to amaze
    Come the mountains and the lakes

Upon me! comes the far stretch'd-out sea,

The most silent home of things most free,

And the rocks o'er whose platforms wind the miles,

And the tarns dark beneath savage piles,

And, betwixt the foamless friths, the blue and

  stilly Isles!

The gull calls hoarsely for its prey

 About me; can it dare

Even as much as flap its wings on its way

 Through so voiceless a vast air?

Yes! it only thinks for its food,

And is like to the islesman rude,

Whose soul with its fog ever foils

Sun and lightning; who in squalor aye toils,

Nor looketh above his peat to eagles of the Isles.

Too weak he is for scenes like this,

 Nor for laughter made, nor tears,

Where no part is as strange as Love's kiss
   Of all the seventy years.
Faint is Summer, pale her love, the Sun ;
Here thunder and music are as one,
When the cloud meets the wave on the kyles,
And it seems as though the rocks would be spoils
Of the storm, when wild Death pours his vial on
     the Isles.

But not more I seek the fruit of stormy waves
   Than that of sunny leas,
I, one of summer pilgrims who stay staves
   'Mid the iron-blue Hebrides,
And gaze, while the loneliness brings awe,
On the ocean-glass which only wings flaw,
When the sea-bird whom the pale Sun beguiles,
While no spray from his rocky nest recoils,
Riots seaward fast and far, and leaves the lifeless
     Isles.

ST. BRIAVELS.

WHEN the weary, hateful town,
  And the wheels round me for miles,
And the hastening up and down
  Of the base whom gain beguiles;
And the roar of rushing trade,
  And the smoke that is its breath,
And its insolence, have made
. My soul faint, nigh unto death—
Times have been when a mere name
To my soul with solace came;
And that name that, like church bells
Now and then heard, with me dwells,
Is thy name, St. Briavels.

Little town, near to the Wye,
  Though I know of thee no more,

K

I desire not ere I die
　　Thee to visit and explore;
For, O village of the saint,
　　Thou it may be dost not claim
Aught of dreamy, sweet, or quaint,
　　Save by music of thy name:
Folly 'tis, and 'twill be harm
Sifting such a vague sweet charm;
So I will not risk the spells
Which might break, my soul foretells,
If I saw St. Briavels.

Yet it must be fair, thy site,
　　'Mid few men and many flowers;
Far away from city's blight,
　　One could dream away the hours,
Gazing on thy bowery plains
　　And blue border-heights, nor tire
Of the orchards, and hill-chains,
　　And the quiet western shire.

Lovers in thee should be blest,

And thy weary ones have rest;

Lightly should their last two ells

Lie of earth on those whose knells

Rung are at St. Briavels.

Though, with time, our hate grows cold,

   And our love might ne'er have been;

Yet sometimes our memories hold

   Faces we but once have seen.

—Place and face have difference none,

   Towns there are my memories tread

Never now, where years agone

   I had scarce erred, blindfolded;—

These,—their names with death have part,

Thine,—but once seen on a chart,—

Lives, nor time's aye-flowing wells

Drown the dream that still compels

Thought of thee, St. Briavels.

"ONLY A WOMAN'S HAIR."

"ONLY a woman's hair!"—
   Well, once, I will confess,
Not all the wealth of a millionnaire
   Could have won from me this tress.

It was won—ay, when was it won?—
   In the days of long ago,
And of all strange places under the sun,—
   At an agricultural show!

We were gazing, arm in arm,
   In a study of love's bright brown,
At a pair of pigeons;—a sudden alarm,
   Her hair was coming down!

We gain'd an ante-room;
    Scarce had I closed the door;
When it fell, in masses of glossy gloom,
    That half way reach'd the floor.

A rosy torch of June
    Was her face, as she hurriedly bound
The dishevell'd strays that her beauty's noon
    With wandering arms enwound.

And I ask'd—ere a day's escape
    Came a scented note and my suit—
" From those rich, ripe clusters one tiny grape
    Is not forbidden fruit?"

    *   *   *   *   *

I " assisted "—('tis Virgil's term)—
    Last week at the very same show,
As a partner in the implement firm
    Of Mangel, Wurzel, and Co.

And I saw Mrs. Tomkinson,
   With ten darlings little and big,
A stoutish lady, intent upon
   A remarkably fine prize pig.

I thought of the sweet lang syne,
   And I dare say so did she ;
But I merely remark'd that the day was fine,
   And ask'd after Mr. T.

Here, Thomas, pull off this boot,
   And fling that rubbish—no, stay !
Tho' Time has taken my hair for his loot,
   And her glossy tresses are grey :

Yet *this* lock never grows sere,
   I gaze, and she shines again,
The star of my youth's most golden year,
   And not the mother of ten !

RYDALMERE.

THINE are no waters wide or wild,
No legend of past smiles or sighs,
No circle to the eye up-piled
Of hills o'er hills that rise.

Yet chose the thoughtfullest great soul
That e'er to verse his spirit gave,
To dwell betwixt thy mighty knoll
And wood-reflecting wave.

And with thy woods, within thy breast,
His quiet memory seems to brood;
Thou little lake, the quietest
Of the fair sisterhood !

THE COLLEGE TUTOR.

YES! Life was like the Morning in her bloom,
    That grows as from high hills she hasteneth
        down;
Nor knew the Queen of sorrows, Memory, whom
    The ashen grey years crown;

Nor that the power was transient of the smiles
    Of the fair rival queen, Euphrosyne,
As morning's gift of sheen to the cloud-isles
    Which float in Heaven's blue sea.

Golden the legend was of life, unread
    In the bright scroll the dark page of the grave,
What time my careless student-days were sped
    Where willow stoops to wave.

The days when love was hope ! where first the
    spires—
Crowning fair Learning's garden still in bud—
Flash on the stranger in the sun's low fires,
    Her father's cottage stood.

Oh ! my soul's life that was one long, sweet sigh,
    Well I recall it, though some hairs are grey,
Well we recall the years, Pauline and I,
    When every month was May.

Yes ! I remember thy fond bosom's pant,
    Seems thy young bloom to touch my shoulder
      still,
When what I urged thy pride refused to grant .
    Against my parents' will.

And many a year has fled, nor brought me change
    Of place—I kneel in the same hall of prayer,
My feet beside the same slow river range,
    Climb the same College stair.

Yet change is mine; more than when day to
    night
  Turns, as by magic, on the tropic wave,
Which was, one moment, as the throne of light,
    And is, the next, its grave.

Or when the love of passion (not like ours
    Whose bloom sweet Heaven makes fadeless, spite
       of fate)
Shows, in a trice, the poison of its flowers,
    And dies—to live as hate.

Or when the mist on mountains, sudden-rent,
    Turns the blank tracts, as fast away it trails,
Into the brows of giants, imminent
    O'er emeraldine vales.

Or when the Eastern Caliph and his love
    Reach'd the dim halls at last of their desire,
Nor had their prize, but sentence aye to rove
    With hands on hearts of fire.

Greater my gradual change than these; the
    dreams
  Are gone that made me as a god at times,
As hammer sounding upon metal seems
  The ringing of life's chimes.

Scarce the most restless, whom no land or tide
  Knows not, have, with the years, forgotten more
Than I, the lonely scholar who abide
  'Mid willows, and with lore.

Springs turn the earth to flowers, to song the
    grove,
  Transform to blue and white the weather grey,
Yet listless is my soul to sweetness of
  Violet, to bird's virelay.

But one thing have I of the old far years,
  One bridge my autumn and my spring between;
A bridge of sighs, to thee I think of tears,
  Our hopeless love, Pauline.

Thus live we, you and I, a league us parts,
   And to the cottage of my faded flower
Sometimes I fare, and there our broken hearts
   We bind up for an hour.

Walking with steps that once more lightly met,
   Or talking by your father's fireside blaze,
We, to whom life has only given regret,
   And length of sober days.

In thy locks and in mine grey strands there are,
   Yet thy thinn'd tresses tie me to the spot
Where once their affluence hid my shoulder,—ah!
   Those hours are unforgot!

WITH lips too happy for laughter,
    Songs sweeter than sirens sing,
And winds that soften'd to waft her,
    And violet eyes, came Spring.

"O Summer, Summer, Summer!"
    I cried when the spring was gone,
My cry for the next newcomer
    Was vain, and the days went on.

She came, indeed, but I knew not;
    She went, and I waited, till
The bud should bloom, but it blew not,
    The music should sound, it was still.

A wan ghost stood beside me
  At last, after many days,
Tear-fill'd were her eyes that eyed me,
  Her voice had no lilt of lays.

The wreath she wore nigh mask'd her,
  With its falling leaves. " Art thou
The ghost of Spring?" I ask'd her,
  " Or is Autumn with me now?"

" But they sing that the spirit dances
  Of Autumn, uplift with wine,
That earth guards her with golden lances,
  While she keeps state under the vine."

" Nay," she answer'd, " thy life rolls onward,
  It is better to grieve than forget,
Through tears must men gaze sunward,
  Give thanks for my gift, regret.

" Thine heart is no rocky splinter,

Thy soul has not lost its wing,

Who has memory of spring in winter,

Has hope of an endless spring."

LORTON VALE.

MY wandering steps went where,
    'Mid hills the clouds that scale,
I met a maiden fair
    In Lorton Vale,

And pass'd upon my path,
    Through such a mist as fills
Full oft that valley's strath,
    And hides the hills.

I saw the fields hard by,
    And through the vapour peer'd
Glimpses of hill-sides nigh,
    Vast, grey, and weird.

Elsewhere the mist hid all,
　　I traced a rook's near flight,
But only by its call,
　　Hoarse in the height.

The springs of Nature's grace
　　To my eyes' thirst were seal'd;
I saw no stream's white race,
　　No fern that reel'd,

Swept by the mountain breeze,
　　Nor the long bowery lea,
Nor the high hill-ash trees,
　　Nor the far sea.

Yet, if that girl made stir
　　My heart where mists did sail,
It was from meeting her
　　In Lorton Vale!

L

The hazard of the world,
 The triumph of the hour,
Fortune upon me hurl'd
 In Danae shower,—

Seem'd falsest spells which Love
 With one brief flash made fail,
Because *his* charm was wove
 In Lorton Vale.

Yet Lorton Vale around,
 (Shepherds have never driven
Flocks o'er a fairer ground),
 Was hid, as Heaven.

Is glory made by gloom
 More glorious?—He whose mind
Recover'd Eden's bloom
 In verse, was blind.

If the wide mist, to please
    My eyes, itself had rent,
Till they, like Lorton bees,
    With sweets were spent;

If I had view'd the heights
    Where lingers day's last fire,
Where wildly the wind smites
    His loudest lyre;

If, clear, the valley's sheet
    Had stretch'd from peak to shore
Its league of flocks that bleat
    And bees that soar;

If not a rood between
    The eagle and the sail,
Had from me hidden been
    In Lorton Vale;

If the last misty wreath
    Had trail'd up, and away ;
Should I have drawn my breath
    In Heaven that day ?

Would the loud world have seem'd
    As a forgotten tale,
While I so sweetly dream'd
    In Lorton Vale?

*   *   *   *   *

I know but this—my soul
    Was painter to my eyes,
The mist hid not a knoll
    Of Paradise.

For plain and mountain slope
    Were lit, not from earth's sky,
With a strange light—of Hope
    Or Memory.

And in it I saw Love,

  A vision pure and pale,

A flower that only throve

  In Lorton Vale.

THE STOUT CRICKETER.

NOT of that sort is he
    Which lounges by the tents to kill
The time with levity;
    Nor loudly boastful of his skill
Telling how, (in a match you didn't see,)
    He drove a slow for six, or smote to leg
A four, or cut a three,
    Or over a tent-peg
Tumbled, but made his catch;—not boastful thus
Is the STOUT CRICKETER, nor frivolous.

Yet you may see him smile
    At his own joke, may hear him air his wits
Most pointlessly and slowly, while
    Heavily on a bench he sits

Smoking a pipe, and with a critic's gaze
   Upon the younger batsmen of his side,
Recalls old cricket memories from the haze
   Of time, not loudly to deride
But calmly to disparage the wild play
" Which, sir, the youngsters of the present day—"

" Smith !" " where's old Smith ?" " now Smith !"
   For innings Smith doth boune ;
In waistcoat black and beltless trousers, with
   His braces not let down,
He, walking stumpwards, doth the lean earth lard;
   His gloves, or, as he funnily calls them, " mits,"
Are button'd by the umpire, he takes guard,
   Most likely on his bat then gravely spits,
Plays the first balls with not untroubled mien,
   But somehow scrapes a score up, say fifteen.

He bowls—swift underhand,
   And has been seen to previously apply—

As though he some mysterious magic plann'd—
  The ball unto his eye.
A smile, yea, e'en a chuckle from him breaks,
  When with a lucky length he floors the stumps;
Off then his hat, his head to rub, he takes,
  Shows how he pitch'd the ball where the ground
    bumps;
But piteous looks, and stolidly perplex'd,
If his " best pitch " " just suits " the man who
    comes in next.

At dinner he is great,
  Drinks beer and sherry, pays for a friend's
    wine;
Grows genial, and proceeds to state
  " He ne'er yet saw a ball so fine
As that which bowl'd him;" liberal then
  He " stands " the umpire's dinner, nor yet stays
His generous hand, but for four seedy men,
  Who somehow claim a dinner, next he pays.

These losels help him, struggling, to get peel'd,

When he, alack! must after dinner field.

Sometimes on tented plain,

    The only veteran there,

I have seen him, running, mirthful plaudits gain

    From athlete youth, or girl-spectators fair;

And I have pitied him as seeming strange,

    Misplaced among the rest, to him mere boys,

And fear'd his memories might sadly range

    Back to fled youth and unreturning joys;

But these fine fancies don't, I think, occur

To my respectable STOUT CRICKETER.

THE WEST TO THE EAST.

THE hyacinths upon my hills!
    You vow'd me like them purely free;
My vales the pride of lilies fills,
    Such pride you turn'd to love in me;
You kiss'd and went, from fresh and fair
I faded, and the rustic squires repair
To shrines more kind than mine to a less stammer'd
        prayer.

Too high it tower'd, and fell, the pride,
    Which should but point to Heaven's high
        dome;
Now village children haunt my side,
    My mountain valley seems my home,

And Time has still'd the secret sigh,

Replaced those grey far flats once brought so

    nigh,

And made appear a dream your love which was

    a lie.

PROSERPINE.

SHE sitteth, sullen-seeming, for her lips
    Are sweet, yet smile not, gay was once their
        smile
And careless where the bee still sips
    Crocus, in Sicily's isle.

Where Enna's summer-silence driven by mirth
    Of her and her flower-finding peers away,
Return'd, when suddenly up from earth,
    Scattering the flowers as spray,

The lord of Hades leapt on his black steeds,
    And dark as tempest, swift as its fierce flame,
Towards Proserpine, along the meads,
    The rushing chariot came.

Whereat, recovering breath, those girls let fall
  Their flower-baskets, and fled shrieking o'er
Their vale of wandering festival,
  Hell's flower-hidden door.

And light white feet of some bled o'er the hills
  Against the sharp stones, fleeing up to where
Fern-forests hide the racing rills,
  And clouds as gauze seem rare.

And some by lily-paven pools below—
  With speed such as saved Daphne o'er the sod
From him who had dropp'd his golden bow—
  Escaped the sterner god.

But taking heart, as by no chase beset,
  The climbers turn'd, and left the slopes of shale
Above them, and their fellows met,
  Now rallying in the vale.

And all sought Proserpine, the sole one miss'd,
   Calling out " Proserpine ! Proserpine !"—in
      vain ;—
They shall haunt Enna when they list,
   But *she*, ah, ne'er again !

Whom, torn from summer and its arch of vair,
   Dim Desolation girds, Night overwhelms,—
Where fire takes place of flowers, there
   Her state is, and her realms.

She in that land where earth's night were as morn,
   Sits in severity without relief,
Far from the first green mist of corn,
   And the last golden sheaf,

Far from where summer covers happy men
   Ever with drifting white and steadfast blue,
Far from eve's hour most heavenly, when
   Love to its tryst is true.

Far from the wondering child and trembling bride,
   From grey hairs honour'd by surrounding breath,
From sweet things smiled and sweeter sigh'd,
   From life far;—and from death.

Far from the countless, restless, human bees,
   Far from the many, far too from the one,
From weary wandering Hercules,
   And falling Phaethon.

From foes remember'd and forgotten friends,
   From the fierce birth and faint death of desire,
From summer's golden dream that ends
   Always in cloud and fire.

From those who pray for peace and have it not,
   From those who whet their swords still for
      the wars,
From all the mystery of the lot
   Cast betwixt sea and stars.

Remote from these, no more she gives redress
   To pluck'd flowers, wreathing them her brows
      to bind,
Her shadowy hair and motionless
   Forgets the sun and wind.

Day from her eyes and laughter from her ears,
   And music's memory from her soul, have gone;
One darkness-piercing sound she hears,
   The roar of Acheron

Ravening around!—her lord she scarcely owns,
   Lurid beside her; silence is between
The ebon everlasting thrones
   Of Hades' king and queen.

Only sometimes she lifts the glooms that lash
   Her lids, and fondly turns to him her eyes;
The intervals betwixt each flash
   Of love, are centuries.

    *   *   *   *   *

Not alone she in Sicily did resign
   Speed of the hours and youth's sweet dream
      and gay,
Here where the world lost Proserpine,
   It lost Rosalia.

Who, in the midmost laughter of her morn,
   When every lute in all the land was her's,
Of her bright beauty made forlorn
   The amorous islanders.

A nunnery seal'd that fountain which the dance
   Once would let loose to shame the sun's full
      blaze,
And turn'd the song and quick shy glance
   To hymn and upward gaze.

And on that isle, while light and shade fleck even
   To the blue tideless waves, its asphodel,
Fame shall bestow the bride of Heaven,
   Fable the queen of Hell.

IN THE LAND OF WORDSWORTH.

YES! I remember,—fix'd, as fate;
    Treasured, as long-kept tress or glove;
Sweet, as revenge; and passionate,
    Yet pure, as truest love;
Dear, as a bride;—stays with me, and shall
        stay,
The memory of one world-obliterating day!

Valleys in which the wind was dead,
    Hills on which it to death was nigh;
—As underfoot, so overhead,
    The triumph of July!

Which heaven with universal blue confess'd,
And hill with streamless flank, and lake with
　　azure rest.

The banners of the clouds were furl'd
　　And stored away, such heat as stills
The singing birds, oppress'd the world
　　Of long vales and high hills;
No sound save of the bee, I, free from men,
Heard, drinking summer's wine in a gorse-
　　cushion'd glen.

Nature, who only seems a name
　　To most of those who come and go,
While she remains and is the same,
　　Nor bodily change doth know,
Now tempest-cloak'd, now dight with star-wreath
　　drawn
Off, when her deep dark hair grows golden with
　　the dawn :—

She who has voices many, and all
    Music to the attunèd ear,
From thunder to the winds that call
    The spring forth; she drew near,
Splendid, with silent-fervent lips, and smiled,
And took me in her arms, as mother takes a
        child.

She, the great mother, Nature! veil'd,
    —But I was given her face to see,
And something with her breath inhaled
    Of immortality,
Or did I dream ?—while the long summer day
Shadowless, windless, bright, pass'd, like an hour,
        away.

Standing above quaint Hawkshead town,
    And Esthwaite's lake of flawless glass,
On the long valley looking down
    From high heath-purpled grass;

More sweetness than the bee there ever sips,
I, hanging on them, heard from those immortal
     lips.

Such sweetness was it to my drouth
    As of the stream where Memory dies.—
Said I, I hung upon her mouth?
    Rather, I read her eyes,
For she being silent that day near the lake,
By splendour and by heat—yea, by her silence—
     spake.

" I alone stay 'twixt sea and sky,"
    (The speech of her deep eyes ran thus,)
" Mine is all visible victory
    O'er the victorious,
For I, I only stand before the breath,
That all things else lays low, of devastating
     Death.

" I only on the sea of Time,
    Of which the billows are the years,
Sail without wreck—I am sublime
    O'er laughter and o'er tears,
For my wrath is not men's wrath, nor with
        them
Rejoice I, when shines forth the sun, my diadem.

" Beauty, the red rose, not at war
    With Innocence the white, and Truth
Amidst them,—these three sisters are
    Of my unfading youth ;
But not my kin are those, the still-miss'd scope
Of amorous hearts of men,—sad Memory and glad
        Hope.

" My son ! I lift thee in mine arms,
    For thee my soul's Æolian strings
I strike, away the music charms
    Men's discords—as on wings

I bid thee soar and give thee Lethe, wet,

Aye, on my lips, that thou the mean world mayst

     forget."

With this she stoop'd, but ere she reach'd

   My mouth, the fantasy was gone;

Though still the blue day, cloud-unbleach'd,

   With halcyon wings flew on,

But purpler hills, and air that ceased to burn,

Told that the light now flow'd from a nigh empty

     urn.

The solemn evening, with its bloom,

   Came, kind to labour and to love,

Flushing Helvellyn's topmost coomb

   High the great hills above;

Thus for me, rapt betwixt the heights and

     bowers,

Ended that lapse serene of memorable hours.

Ended, and left me of my lot
   Weary, and of blind man's desire,—
To those who conquer envying not
   The laurel and the lyre,
But to the hill-moths brown, their fate,—to
      wing
Life's flutter all away on these red lawns of
      ling.

THE END.

CHISWICK PRESS:—PRINTED BY WHITTINGHAM AND WILKINS,
TOOKS COURT, CHANCERY LANE.

www.ingramcontent.com/pod-product-compliance
Lightning Source LLC
Chambersburg PA
CBHW020227030726
47497CB00009B/2977